"Ho, ho!" chuckled Jolly Old Santa Claus, as he stroked his long white beard. And then he began laughing all over again, his eyes twinkling and merry.

"Come, little brownies . . . come, my dear Mrs. Santa," he called . . . "for this is a very wonderful letter indeed."

Mrs. Santa Claus, who had been playing the piano while the little brownies sang their favorite Christmas songs, stopped — and she, too, came to see this letter.

"What does it say?" "Who is it from?" "Did a little boy or a little girl write it?" "Where is it from?" "Did the . . ."

"Whoa there, just a moment, my fine little friends," said Jolly Old Santa Claus. "One question at a time, or I can't hear any of you."

"Yes," he chuckled, "it is a letter from a little boy who has been very good all year. He has minded his Mommy and Daddy, has been very helpful to his brothers and sisters, kind to his little dog and cat, and . . . can you guess what he wants to know?"

The little brownies all tried to guess. "Will he get a train for Christmas?" "Will we find his new house?" "Will it snow on Christmas Eve?"

"No, no — you'll never guess," chuckled Jolly Old Santa Claus . . . "this good little boy wants to know if we are busy getting ready for Christmas at the North Pole!"

"Are we!!" shouted all the little brownies. "We most certainly are . . ."

The North Pole is the busiest place just before Christmas . . . little brownies are working away making all kinds of wonderful toys, baking goodies for the boys and girls and . . .

. . . But, come with me, and we'll "peek" in at the North Pole, and then you can see what is happening. Would you like that?

But remember, you must be very quiet, for no one can disturb the little brownies or they will never finish all their work before Christmas Eve.

"Go along," said Jolly Old Santa Claus, "but you must remember to be very, very good . . . and don't let the brownies see you."

First, let's stop at the Cookie Kitchen and see what is happening, shall we?

Just *look* at the little brownies scurrying about, with great smudges of flour on their aprons, sugar on their hands . . .

And see how hard they are working!

Oops! Old "Gram'pa Brownie" just fell; the big sack of flour is very heavy, and he was trying to walk backwards into the kitchen! And you know, he *never* remembers to wear his spectacles, he forgets them all the time!

And look at "Jingles," sitting way on top of the oven, telling the brownies just how to place the trays of cookies so they won't burn.

Star-shaped cookies — heart-shaped cookies — gingerbread cookies — round and fat little cookies.

Oh! it's such fun to make these sugar cookies for all the good little boys and girls to enjoy.

Aren't you glad when Christmastime comes and *you* can eat such good things?

But, we must hurry on . . . the North Pole is a big place, and there is much to see.

Where would you like to visit next? I know . . . the Toy
Shop! And, so it is.

Isn't this a wonderful place? Did you know that it would
look like this?

Every brownie is busy. All of them, that is, except "Lazy
Brownie." He's *always* playing. Just look at him — riding
the rock-a-bye pony when he should be helping.

Shame! But Jolly Old Santa Claus will soon see him at
play again, for he knows all about his little brownies.

Right now, he is busy checking his list of toys . . .
airplanes — trains — drums — building blocks — dolls —
teddy bears — rubber bouncing balls —

Goodness! There are so many toys to finish before Christmas! It's fun to look around the Toy Shop, isn't it?

Can you see "Lady Whiskers" . . . Jolly Old Santa Claus' favorite cat? And do you see "Merry One," falling down the stairs? I think old Jack-in-the-box frightened him, don't you?

And look at the clock on the wall!

"Chief Brownie" has seen it, too, and he is telling the brownies to hurry . . . it's getting late, and Christmas will soon be here!

While the little brownies in the Toy Shop finish painting and fixing all the toys, let's see what they are doing in the "Christmas Tree Room."

Oh, ho! . . . isn't this a beautiful room! Have you ever
seen so many bright colors . . . or so many pretty
ornaments for the Christmas trees?

And look! . . . back there in the corner . . . they are
blowing the bubbles to make the ornaments!

And over there — near the box of sand — there's "Impy
Brownie" dipping the ornaments into beautiful paint to
color them.

This is a very special job, and only the most careful
brownies can work here, for the glass ornaments have to
be handled very carefully or they will break.

Did you see "Lady Whiskers," too? She's sitting way up
high on the rafters, watching the brownies . . . for if she
walked on the floor, her long tail might break the
ornaments, and "Chief Brownie" wouldn't like that at all!

And look at "Lazy Brownie" . . . not working, again. Shame! He's sitting way up high, too, on top of the tool shelf, so no one can see him. But, it won't be long before Jolly Old Santa Claus sees him, and then he'll be working.

Doesn't Santa Claus look happy? He thinks his little brownies have made such beautiful ornaments.

It won't be long before Santa Claus is tip-toeing into your house to decorate your Christmas tree.

It's getting closer and closer to Christmastime!

We must hurry on now and see all of the shops, for it will soon be time to leave.

Where is Jolly Old Santa Claus going?

Let's follow him, shall we?

Why, this is the office of Jolly Old Santa Claus, isn't it? It must be — for look! There is his desk, and there is Santa Claus, reading the letters from good little boys and girls.

And there on the wall is the list of good little boys and girls and bad little boys and girls, too. Oh, look! "Helper Brownie" is putting a mark under "Bad Little Boys and Girls." But, I hope it won't be for you!

And Mrs. Santa Claus is marking the names and addresses of all little boys and girls who have moved to new houses since last year, so Jolly Old Santa Claus will be sure to find them.

And, couldn't you guess it? "Lady Whiskers" is sitting on top of Santa's chair, and "Lazy Brownie" . . . what is he doing, hiding under Santa's desk and blowing smoke rings? That brownie . . . he's always getting into some mischief, isn't he?

But, see, "Jingles" is busy handing letters to "Impy Brownie" to give Santa to read.

And "Chief Brownie" is busy tugging in the great heavy sack of letters for Santa to read.

And look at Santa Claus . . . doesn't he look happy? He must be reading a letter from a *very* good little boy or girl. Maybe it is your letter . . . do you think it is?

But, we must scurry along, for Santa Claus has just asked "Chief Brownie" if the Christmas trees are all ready. And that means Christmas is really coming!

And, it looks as though they *are* all ready, doesn't it?

Christmas trees . . . Christmas trees . . . all over the forest. Have you ever seen such beautiful trees? And, won't they look lovely after Jolly Old Santa Claus and his helpers have decorated them with the pretty glass ornaments!

See the little brownies sawing the trees.

And look at the little animals in the forest! How they love to watch the brownies collecting the trees, for they whistle and sing the happiest songs! You can hear their singing wherever you walk in the forest.

Did you see "Old Gram'pa Brownie" slip in the deep snow? And look, he's lost his cap! He's the funniest brownie, isn't he? He just *never* remembers to wear his spectacles!

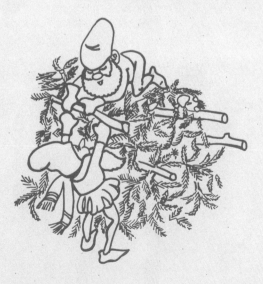

I wonder where "Lazy Brownie" is. He's probably not working at all, but talking to the reindeer. Can you see him anyplace?

It won't be long now, before Jolly Old Santa Claus will be ready to leave the North Pole and then, it really will be "almost" Christmastime.

While the busy little brownies finish loading the trees into the sleigh, let's see what Mrs. Santa Claus is doing.

There she is . . . in front of Santa's castle, checking to see
that everything will be ready so Jolly Old Santa Claus can
leave on time.

The toys are being put into the sleigh, and look at the teddy
bear. He's so big that *two* brownies have to carry him into
the sleigh.

"Chief Brownie" has Santa's Route List in his hand, and
will know just where the reindeer must stop.

And "Jingles" is bringing the reindeer out to tie them to the
sleigh.

Look what Mrs. Santa Claus is holding in her hands! She has ear-muffs and a heavy scarf, so Santa Claus will be warm on his long trip tonight.

For tonight is the night. At long last it is here. It is the night before Christmas!

You must be very quiet now and hop into bed quickly, for Santa Claus is ready to leave.

The stars are twinkling in the blue sky above and all the world is hushed and still, waiting for this magical night.

For tonight, yes, tonight is the night he comes!

Swiftly through the skies they will fly . . . Jolly Old Santa Claus and his eight reindeer.

And more quietly than softly falling snow, he will land atop your house. And then, silently — oh, so silently — he will put a pack of toys on his back and slide down the chimney . . .

He will fill your stocking with goodies . . . trim your Christmas tree with beautiful ornaments . . . and underneath the tree . . . what wonderful surprises there will be!

And then, just as quietly . . . and just as quickly as he came . . . in the wink of an eye, he will be gone.

All through the night he will go, bringing happiness and joy and love into the homes of all good little children.

And long before the sun rises in the Christmas morning sky, Jolly Old Santa Claus will have visited the homes of every good little boy and girl all over the world, and will be flying back to his home in the North Pole.

And such excitement there will be when he comes!

The little brownies will want to know all about Jolly Old
Santa Claus' trip.

"Did it snow, Santa Claus?" "Was it very cold?" "Were the
good little boys and girls happy with their toys?" "Were
they all fast asleep in their beds?"

But, look at "Lady Whiskers!" She has a surprise for Jolly
Old Santa Claus, too . . . four soft, cuddly little kittens.
And, aren't they cute little kittens?

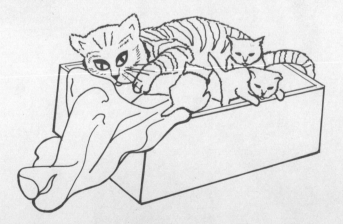

While the little brownies feed the reindeer and settle them down for sleep, Jolly Old Santa Claus will begin to tell them all about his trip.

And what a wonderful trip it was.

But listen . . . isn't that Mrs. Santa Claus calling to Jolly Old Santa Claus and the little brownies?

Yes, it is Mrs. Santa Claus calling, and oh, how very wonderful this looks!

Mrs. Santa Claus has made cups of hot chocolate and sweet cookies for Santa and the brownies, for he is very tired, and very hungry, after his long night's journey.

And, the brownies are tired and hungry, too.

Now they are *all* busy little brownies . . . even "Lazy Brownie" who is busy shining Santa Claus' boots and polishing the jingle bells from his sleigh.

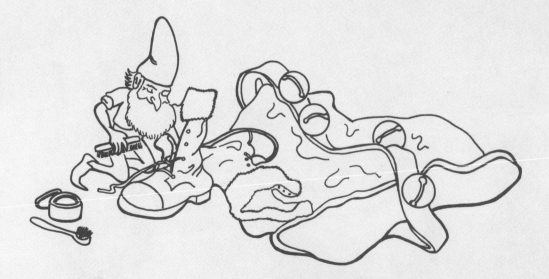

"Chief Brownie" is telling his helpers to pack the toys very carefully, for they can be used next year.

And look at "Impy Brownie" . . . spilling the bucket of red paint! It's the excitement of Santa Claus coming back from his trip.

But soon, very soon, all of the work will be finished.

And then, Jolly Old Santa Claus and Mrs. Santa Claus will rest and visit awhile, and start making their plans for next Christmas.

And the little brownies . . . what will they do?

Why, after they have eaten all the delicious cookies that Mrs. Santa Claus has made for them, it will be their bedtime.

And what tired little brownies they are . . . for they have worked very hard baking Christmas cookies . . . collecting trees . . . making beautiful ornaments and pretty toys . . . getting everything ready for your Christmas.

But first, just before it is bedtime, they will have a big pillow fight . . . for they always do this on the night of Santa's return.

And such merriment and such fun!

And then . . . when the brownies are safely tucked into their little beds, Jolly Old Santa Claus and Mrs. Santa Claus will tiptoe into their bedroom . . . and, standing at the bottom of the winding stairs, they will call "good night" to their little brownie friends . . .

And, as they reach the bedroom door, they will turn off the light . . . throw a big kiss to the little brownies, and then . . .

Quietly . . . oh, so quietly . . . it is almost a tiny whisper . . . you can hear all the little brownies, and Mrs. Santa Claus and Jolly Old Santa Claus as they call to each and every good little boy and good little girl all over the world . . .